First published in Great Britain in 2015 by Andersen Press Ltd.,

20 Vauxhall Bridge Road, London SW1V 2SA.

Copyright © Chris Judge, 2015.

All rights reserved.

Printed and bound in Malta.

2   3   4   5   6   7   8   9   10

British Library Cataloguing in Publication Data available

ISBN 978 1 78344 114 3

THE SNOW
BEAST

CHRIS JUDGE

For
Joey

The Beast was always thrilled when
he woke up to find SNOW.

Every year, on the first day of snow, he helped the mountain villagers to put on a festival to celebrate.

But this year there was a problem.

The Beast carefully climbed down his mountain to the village.

It was in chaos – every tool had been stolen.

"We'll never build our festival now," said an angry villager. "It must be the work of that abominable Snow Beast."

Scratching his head, the Beast promised to find this mysterious monster and get everyone's tools back.

Soon, he came across some big, beastly-looking footprints in the snow.

He followed the footprints

as the snow got deeper

and deeper

and deeper

until finally he was stuck.

So the Beast decided to dig his way through.

Just as he reached higher ground...

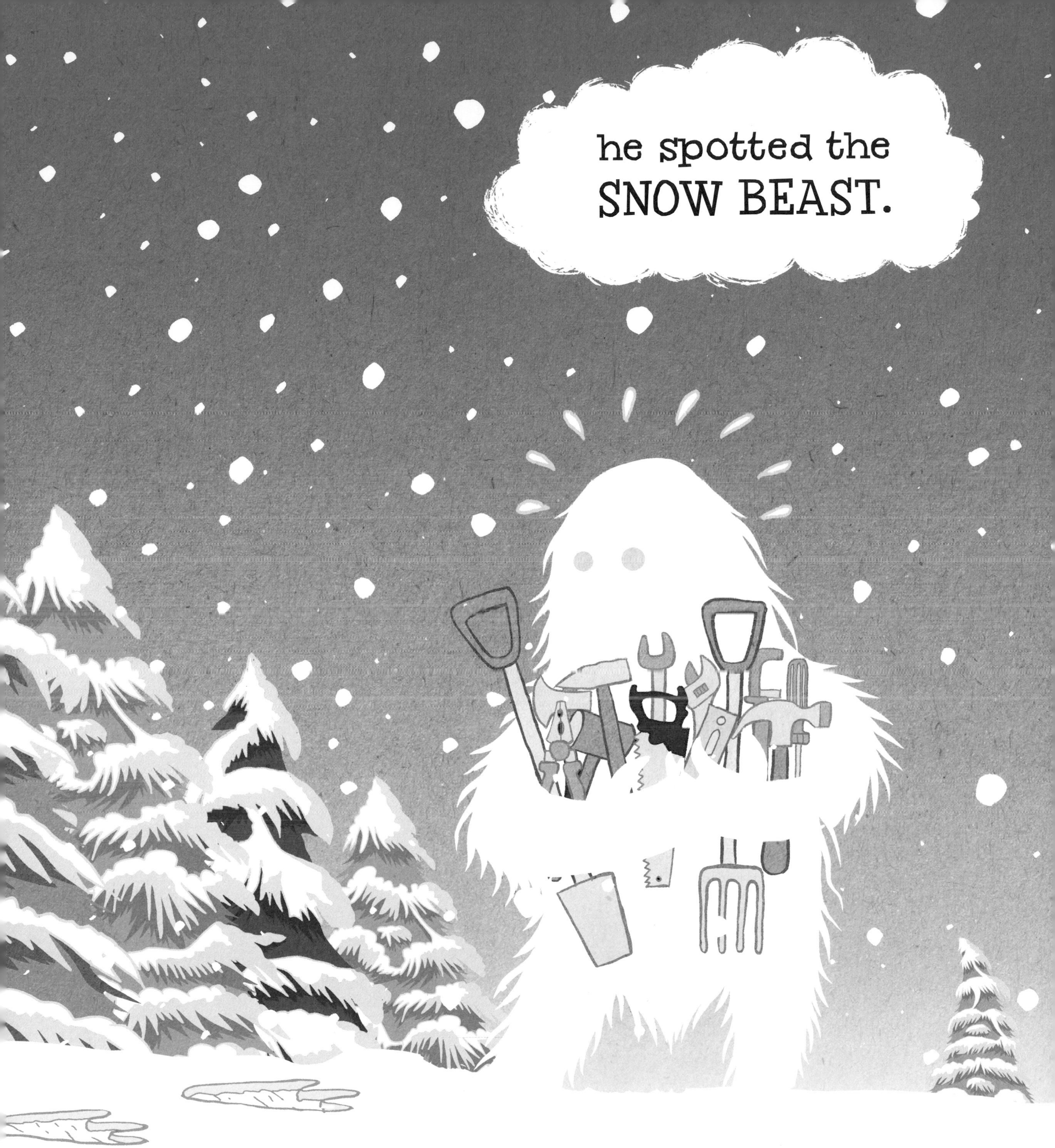
he spotted the
SNOW BEAST.

"Stop, thief!" shouted the Beast.

But the Snow Beast

did not stop.

The Beast decided he needed
extra help to catch this criminal.

Then the chase was on.

But just when it looked as
if the Beast would catch up...

he realised

he should have

learned how

to stop.

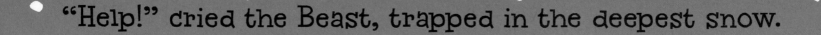

"Help!" cried the Beast, trapped in the deepest snow.

Luckily, someone unexpected came to the rescue.

While the Beast dried off, the Snow Beast
explained that his mobile home had broken down.
He had taken the tools to repair it.
"Maybe I can help?" said the Beast.

As they ran through the snow, the two beasts
found out they had a lot in common.

"You live on an iceberg?" asked the Beast in amazement when they reached the shore.

"Well, not ON an iceberg," replied the Snow Beast.

"IN an iceberg."

The Beast
couldn't believe
his eyes as his
new friend showed him
around his home.
"The big blue propeller is
broken," explained the Snow Beast,
as they reached the engine room.

"No problem," said the Beast.
"I can fix this in a jiffy."

The Snow Beast was
very happy indeed.

He offered to return all
the tools straight away.

The Beast was so excited about introducing
his new friend to everybody

that he ran too fast,

tumbled down the mountain

and **crashed** into the village.

"No, no – it's me," said the Beast,
shaking off the snow.

The villagers breathed a sigh of relief.

"No, no - this is my friend," said the Beast and he told the villagers about his adventure.

The Snow Beast returned everybody's tools and said he was very, very sorry.

The villagers forgave him, even the angry one,
but it was too late to put on the snow festival.

"Hmmmm..." said the Beast.
"I think I might have an idea."